For Tufta and Plud, with all my love — Dawn

For my little monster, Alfie, and my big monster, Tim — Kate

All rights reserved. Published by Chicken House, an imprint of Scholastic Inc.,
Publishers since 1920. CHICKEN HOUSE, SCHOLASTIC, and associated logos are trademarks
and/or registered trademarks of Scholastic Inc. www.scholastic.com

Library of Congress Cataloging-in-Publication Data
McNiff, Dawn.
Mommy's little monster / written by Dawn McNiff ; pictures by Kate Willis-Crowley.   p. cm.
Summary: Tiny Troll is very unhappy that his mother is leaving him with a babysitter while she
goes to a party for grown-ups. · ISBN 978-0-545-48057-4 · [1. Mother and child – Fiction.
2. Babysitters – Fiction. 3. Trolls – Fiction.] I. Willis-Crowley, Kate, ill. II. Title.
PZ7.M478796Mom 2013 · [E] – dc23 · 2012030539

10 9 8 7 6 5 4 3 2 1   13 14 15 16 17

Printed in China   38
First edition, March 2013

Kate Willis-Crowley used watercolors, gouache, pen, and pencil to create the
artwork for *Mommy's Little Monster*. To give the trolls' caves texture and
depth, she used watercolor washes and pencil. Then she used gouache
and pen to call out the characters and all the "gooey" details!
Body text was set in Burbank Big.
Display text was set in Corndog Clean.

Book design by Chelsea C. Donaldson

Mommy's Little MONSTER

written by **Dawn McNiff** pictures by **Kate Willis-Crowley**

Chicken House
Scholastic Inc. / New York

TROLLS love their mommies.

Tiny Troll loved his mommy a lot.

More than puddles.

More than earwigs.

But Tiny Troll's mommy was going to a party tonight.

"Coming with you!" said Tiny Troll.

"Oh no, my little monster," said his mommy. "This party's only for grown-ups. Mrs. Hag is going to babysit you."

"I'm NOT a baby!" he whined.

But his mommy wouldn't listen.

Tiny Troll sat on his mommy's lap while she painted her claws and curled her bristles.

He held on to her leg while she waxed her tail and rubbed slime into her scales.

Then she dabbed behind her ears with her bluebottle perfume, and put on her high-heeled clodhoppers and her pondweed cloak.

She was ready.

Tiny Troll took one look at his mommy and
loved her so much he nearly popped!

She was the prettiest mommy ever.

She was Princess Mommy Troll.

He put his arms in the air.

His mommy picked him up.

She smelled stinky-sweet and strange—

not like his mommy at all.

Mrs. Hag arrived.

Tiny Troll clung on tight, but his mommy was firm.

She put him back down on the ground.

"Come now, my little monster," she said, "give

Mommy a kiss good-bye."

But Tiny Troll shook his head.

He turned away and pouted.

So his mommy blew him a kiss

and slipped out the cave door.

Tiny Troll roared!

He threw himself at the door.

"Come on, lovey," said Mrs. Hag. "How about

some warm mudmilk and a bedtime story?"

Tiny Troll liked mudmilk.

But no he loved his mommy more.

"NO!" he yelled.

He flung his toy slug against the wall.

"MOMM-Y-Y-Y!"

Swamproom

"Okay," Mrs. Hag said kindly,

"I'll be in the swamproom

if you want me."

Tiny Troll lay with his face scrunched into the itchy mat.

His tears made a big wet patch.

"Meanie Mommy," he muttered.

He drummed the door hard with his tiny tail.

Then he smelled a creamy, muddy smell

coming from the swamproom.

Tiny Troll sighed. He did like mudmilk.

He stood up and wiped his eyes.

He peeped around the door.

"Does mudmilk make crying

go away?" he asked.

"I think it does," said Mrs. Hag.

So Tiny Troll had a mugful of mudmilk, and
Mrs. Hag read him his favorite story about
a little troll scaring a big wolf away.
Then Mrs. Hag let him have ANOTHER mugful.

Tiny Troll snuggled up to her.
His mommy *never* let him have more.

ROCKS

CAVES

SLUGS

Mud

Tiny Troll's eyelids suddenly seemed very heavy.

He felt Mrs. Hag lift him up and carry him to his bog.

She gently tucked him in.

When Tiny Troll woke up, it was still nighttime, and his mommy was leaning over his bed to kiss him good-night. She was still wearing her party dress. But she had taken off her makeup. And her bristles smelled of mold again.

"I'm back home," she said softly. "And I brought you a treat from the party."

It was a bag of rotten worms — his favorite.

Tiny Troll hugged his lovely mommy and his yummy worms and

smiled a sleepy smile. Maybe grown-up parties weren't so bad after all.

"Who'll always be my baby?" she whispered. "Who's Mommy's little monster?"

Tiny Troll said, "Me."

And as his mommy stroked his head, he drifted back to sleep.

Rotten
Worms